Rooftop Garden

WRITTEN BY **Danna Smith**

ILLUSTRATED BY **Pati Aguilera**

SUNG BY **Holly Turton**

Barefoot Books
step inside a story

A rooftop garden is what we need —
Friends and family all agree.
A garden starts with hardy seeds.
A rooftop garden is what we need.

Dig a hole and in they go.

Sow the seeds with a shovel and hoe.

Plant them, pat them, row by row.

Dig a hole and in they go.

Lots of sun and a little shade
Bring lettuce, carrots, mint and sage.
Mark them with the signs we made.
Lots of sun and a little bit of shade.

Water the soil when it gets dry.
Time to wait till — me-oh-my!
Tiny shoots reach for the sky.
Water the soil when it gets dry.

Pull the weeds and make a stack.

Pesky weeds! We fill a sack.

Pick them, pull them, they grow back!

Pull the weeds and let's make a stack.

Garden friends fly to and fro,
Spreading pollen as they go —
Dust that helps the veggies grow.
Garden friends, they fly to and fro.

Grab your gloves and fill a jug.

Gather slimy snails and slugs.

Say goodbye to hungry bugs!

Grab your gloves and fill a bug jug.

Time to harvest our rooftop crop.
Pick and pull and twist — don't stop!
Fill the baskets to the top.
Time to harvest our own rooftop crop.

A garden feast! Oh, what a treat.
Prepare the food and take a seat.
Pass a plate and let's all eat.
A garden feast! Oh, what a treat.

Eight Steps for Growing a Garden

Build a raised garden bed with planks of wood and fill it with fresh soil. Then choose some seeds and follow these steps to grow your own crop! Make sure you also follow the directions that come with your seed packets.

Step 1:
Sow the Seeds

Using a trowel or your finger, dig small holes in a row, making sure there's enough space between them. Plant your seeds in each hole and cover lightly with soil.

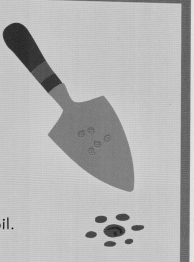

Step 2:
Mark Your Rows

Keep track of the seeds you planted by marking them with a label. Use a stick or recycled strip of plastic for each row, then write the name and the date of when you sowed the seeds.

Step 3:
Water the Soil

Take your watering can and thoroughly water the soil until it's moist. Check on your seeds regularly. When the top of the soil looks and feels dry, water it. The moisture helps the seeds grow into plants.

Step 4:
Pull up the Weeds

Weeds are any plants you do not want growing in your garden. Dig around them and pull up the entire plant, including the roots, to keep them from growing back. Gather the weeds in a bag to throw away or compost them.

Step 5:
Welcome Pollinators

Pollinators like birds, bees and butterflies are animals that move a powder called pollen from flower to flower. This helps the plants grow seeds and fruit. Bring pollinators to your garden by growing flowering plants and providing shelter and water, such as a birdbath, bee hotel or butterfly puddle.

Step 6:
Debug with a Jug

Find hungry snails and slugs when the sun goes down. Grab your gardening gloves and a jug. Put any snails or slugs into your jug and take them to a space where you can safely release them away from your garden.

Step 7:
Harvest Your Crop

When your plants have matured and ripened, it's time to harvest (pick and gather) them. To pick fruits and vegetables, twist them gently where they connect to the stem of the plant.

Step 8:
Prepare Your Feast

There are lots of different ways to prepare food from your garden. You can make soups and salads, smoothies and sauces, and even desserts and baked goods. Whatever you choose, share your feast so others can enjoy the harvest too!

What Do You Want to Grow?

cauliflower

50 to 100 days from seed to harvest

potatoes

70 to 100 days from seed to harvest

watermelons

70 to 85 days from seed to harvest

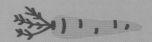

carrots

50 to 80 days from seed to harvest

tomatoes

65 to 85 days from seed to harvest

Six Stages of Plant Growth

Thousands of kinds of plants exist in the world. And while they are all very different, most of them follow the same stages of growth.

Stage 1:
Germination

During **seed** growth, nutrients (materials needed to grow) inside the seed help it sprout. This is called germination.

Stage 2:
Seedling

As a seedling, the **roots** grow down into the soil as green **leaves** grow above the ground.

Stage 3:
Vegetative

Once enough leaves have formed, the **stem** gets taller and the leaves larger as the growth of flower buds begins.

Stage 5:
Flowering

When the **flowers** bloom, pollinators like birds, bees and butterflies visit them to drink nectar (sweet juice) and pick up pollen. Then the flowers fall off and the plant grows fruits or vegetables.

Stage 6:
Ripening

At the final stage, the **fruit** is fully grown, ready to harvest and enjoy!

Stage 4:
Budding

While the plant continues to get bigger, the **flower buds** are getting ready to bloom.

Rooftop Garden

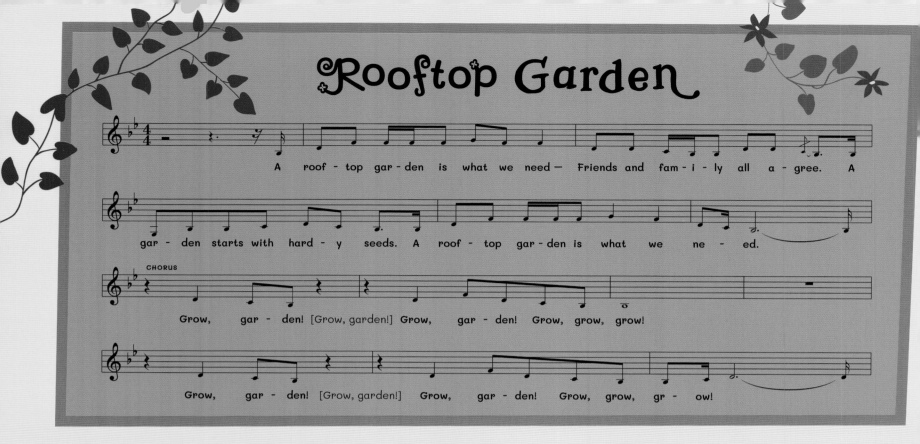

A roof-top gar-den is what we need — Friends and fam-i-ly all a-gree. A gar-den starts with hard-y seeds. A roof-top gar-den is what we ne-ed.

CHORUS

Grow, gar-den! [Grow, garden!] Grow, gar-den! Grow, grow, grow!

Grow, gar-den! [Grow, garden!] Grow, gar-den! Grow, grow, gr-ow!

Barefoot Books would like to thank Francesca Mazzilli, Farm Manager, for her expert input as we developed this book.

Barefoot Books, 23 Bradford Street, 2nd Floor, Concord, MA 01742
Barefoot Books, 29/30 Fitzroy Square, London, W1T 6LQ

Text copyright © 2022 by Danna Smith
Illustrations copyright © 2022 by Pati Aguilera
The moral rights of Danna Smith and Pati Aguilera have been asserted

Lead vocals by Holly Turton. Musical composition, arrangement
and recording © 2022 by Mike Flannery. Produced, mixed and mastered by
Jumping Giant, New York City, USA. Animation by Collaborate Agency, UK

First published in the United States of America by Barefoot Books, Inc
and in Great Britain by Barefoot Books, Ltd in 2022. All rights reserved

Graphic design by Sarah Soldano, Barefoot Books
Edited and art directed by Kate DePalma, Barefoot Books
Educational notes by Bree Reyes, Barefoot Books

Reproduction by Bright Arts, Hong Kong. Printed in China
This book was typeset in Mali and Kidlit
The illustrations were prepared with digital techniques

Hardback ISBN 978-1-64686-495-9 | Paperback ISBN 978-1-64686-496-6
E-book ISBN 978-1-64686-578-9

British Cataloguing-in-Publication Data:
a catalogue record for this book is
available from the British Library

Library of Congress
Cataloging-in-Publication
Data is available under
LCCN 2021949404

1 3 5 7 9 8 6 4 2

Go to *www.barefootbooks.com/rooftopgarden* to access
your audio singalong and video animation online.

Barefoot Books
Step inside a story

At Barefoot Books, we celebrate art and story that opens the hearts
and minds of children from all walks of life, focusing on themes that
encourage independence of spirit, enthusiasm for learning and respect
for the world's diversity. The welfare of our children is dependent on
the welfare of the planet, so we source paper from sustainably managed
forests and constantly strive to reduce our environmental impact.
Playful, beautiful and created to last a lifetime, our products combine
the best of the present with the best of the past to educate our
children as the caretakers of tomorrow.

www.barefootbooks.com

Danna Smith was born with a green thumb having grown up around her family's produce business in Utah, USA. She now plants her garden in northern California, where she lives with her husband and two grown children. Danna is the author of numerous books for kids. Her love of gardening and nature sowed the seed for this book.

As a child, **Pati Aguilera** liked to do all kinds of crafts, draw and spend a lot of time sorting and looking at her pencils. She is Chilean and has lived a large part of her life in the city of Santiago, where she studied design and became a book illustrator. Today she lives in the countryside with her partner and two daughters, and is building the biggest craft project of her life: her own house with a large garden!

Holly Turton is a British vocalist with roots in blues, funk and soul music. When she's not recording, teaching singing in schools or performing live, you can find Holly in her garden, potting plants and vegetables for the upcoming season. She currently lives on the beautiful Cornish coast of England.